Kids Crossword Puzzles Ages 6-8

This book belongs to:

_____

What's the connection? What do a kite, your bunk bed, and your eyes have in common? They're all part of a short story about your eyes playing tricks on you.

It was dark. There seemed to be someone hiding behind your bunk bed. As it turned out it was just your kite and your eyes playing tricks on you.

That's the story behind the words in the first puzzle: Crossword Connection 1. The rest of the stories are up to you.

These puzzles can be used to sharpen language skills and as prompt words to inspire the imagination of young story writers.

First complete all the puzzles. Then pick a puzzle and use the words to write a short story.

Let the fun begin.

Please write a review on Amazon.

Your kind reviews and honest comments help us to create more books like this.

Thank You.

You can find all of our books in our Amazon bookstore here:

https://amazon.com/author/jwpublishing

Crossword Connection 1

Solve the following puzzle based on the clues given!

BUNK   KITE   EYES

Across

[3] A flying toy

Down

[1] A type of bed, double ...
[2] You see with these

Crossword Connection 2

Solve the following puzzle based on the clues given!

ALL   YELLOW   EASY

Across

[2] The color of lemons

Down

[1] Everyone
[3] The opposite of difficult

Crossword Connection 3

Solve the following puzzle based on the clues given!

CUB   MOON   COIN

Across

[2] A bit of metal money

Down

[1] This is seen in the sky at night

[2] A baby lion

Crossword Connection 4

Solve the following puzzle based on the clues given!

END   OPEN   COLD

Across

[1] Not warm
[3] Finish

Down

[2] The opposite of shut

Crossword Connection 5

Solve the following puzzle based on the clues given!

BANK   ARM   DUCK

Across

[2] A place where you can keep your money

Down

[1] Quacking bird

[3] Your hand is on the end of this

Crossword Connection 6

Solve the following puzzle based on the clues given!

ALONE   DEAF   CAMEL

Across

[1] An animal with a hump that lives in the desert

[3] not able to hear

Down

[2] By yourself

Crossword Connection 7

Solve the following puzzle based on the clues given!

FEET   PET   KNEE

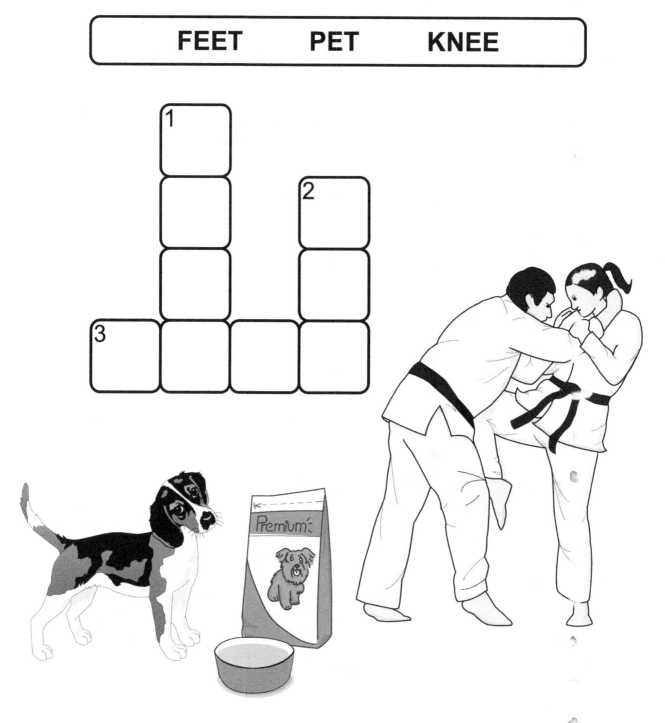

Across

[3] These are at the ends of your legs

Down

[1] The joint in the middle of your leg

[2] A domestic animal that you feed and look after

Crossword Connection 8

Solve the following puzzle based on the clues given!

APPLE   PEA   LAMP

Across

[2] Reading light

[3] Tiny round green vegetable

Down

[1] Crunchy fruit with a core

Crossword Connection 9

Solve the following puzzle based on the clues given!

STOP   ONE   EIGHT

Across

[1] Five, four, three, two, ...

[3] What you must do at a red light

Down

[2] Four plus four

Crossword Connection 10

Solve the following puzzle based on the clues given!

BALL   EAGLE   BIKE

Across

[1] A two-wheeled vehicle with pedals

[3] A bouncy sphere that's fun to kick, hit and catch

Down

[2] The USA uses this bird as its national emblem

Crossword Connection 11

Solve the following puzzle based on the clues given!

SIREN   POPCORN   NEST

Across

[3] A loud warning sound from an ambulance or firetruck vehicle

Down

[1] A popular snack at the movies

[2] A twig home where a baby bird lives

Crossword Connection 12

Solve the following puzzle based on the clues given!

AXE   ACTOR   RUN

Across

[1] This is used to chop wood
[2] Move quickly

Down

[1] One who likes to pretend

Crossword Connection 13

Solve the following puzzle based on the clues given!

HOP   STAMP   OAR

Across

[2] A paddle used to row a boat

[3] Jump up and down on one foot

Down

[1] You put this on a letter before posting it

Crossword Connection 14

Solve the following puzzle based on the clues given!

SAW   HANDYMAN   WOOD

Across

[2] Something you get out of a tree

[3] A wood-cutting tool

Down

[1] A person skilled in doing odd jobs

Crossword Connection 15

Solve the following puzzle based on the clues given!

BEE   CLIMB   BEACH

Across

[1] Where you go to enjoy the sand and surf

Down

[1] Buzzing insect

[2] Go up a tree, or a hill, or a mountain

Crossword Connection 16

Solve the following puzzle based on the clues given!

APE   WEEKDAY   AGO

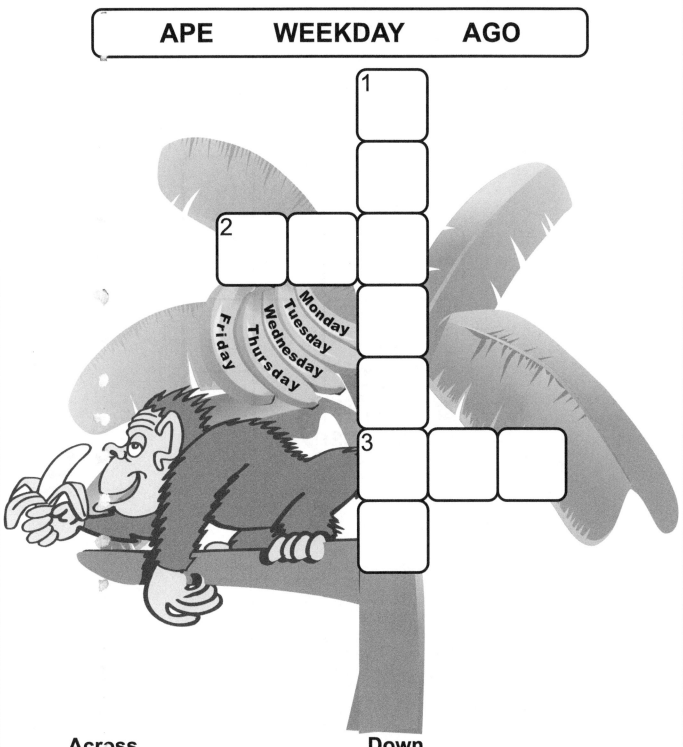

Across

[2] Large monkey

[3] In the past, a long time ...

Down

[1] Monday, Tuesday, Wednesday, Thursday or Friday

Crossword Connection 17

Solve the following puzzle based on the clues given!

ACORN   YES   LEMON

Across

[3] Sour yellow citrus fruit

Down

[1] The seed of an oak tree

[2] Opposite of no

Crossword Connection 18

Solve the following puzzle based on the clues given!

EEL   BADGE   CAR

Across

[2] Four-wheeled family vehicle

[3] A long slippery fish

Down

[1] You pin this on to your shirt

Crossword Connection 19

Solve the following puzzle based on the clues given!

| LID | BOARD | ARM |

Across

[2] The part of your body between your shoulder and hand

[3] The top of a jar, bottle or box

Down

[1] Games such as Chess, Scrabble and Ludo are played on one of these

Crossword Connection 20

Solve the following puzzle based on the clues given!

DRUM **CUP** **DIRT**

Across

[2] An instrument that you hit with sticks to keep the beat

Down

[1] You drink from this

[2] There is lots of this in the garden. It is also called earth

Crossword Connection 21

Solve the following puzzle based on the clues given!

TIDY   SKI   SNOW

Across

[2] A way to move quickly down a snowy mountainside

Down

[1] Neat and with everything in the right place

[2] In cold places this falls to the ground

Crossword Connection 22

Solve the following puzzle based on the clues given!

SAD　　　WALLABY　　　BEAR

Across

[2] Unhappy

[3] Could be a teddy or a grizzly

Down

[1] A small kangaroo-like animal

Crossword Connection 23

Solve the following puzzle based on the clues given!

ROSE   SEEDS   AISLE

Across

[2] This beautiful flower has thorns on its stem

[3] You plant these to grow flowers or vegetables

Down

[1] The passage between seats in a cinema, church or a walkway in a market

Crossword Connection 24

Solve the following puzzle based on the clues given!

BUS   SCAR   SLUG

Across

[2] Slimy slow-moving creature that doesn't have a shell

Down

[1] Something that can take lots of children to school

[2] A mark left on your skin after a wound has healed

Crossword Connection 25

Solve the following puzzle based on the clues given!

DEEP   ANGEL   BATH

Across

[1] A tub that you fill with water and get in to have a wash

[3] If water in a sink is shallow then water in the bath is...

Down

[2] A heavenly being, or what your mum might call you when you are very good

Crossword Connection 26

Solve the following puzzle based on the clues given!

LEGAL   CORE   SUNNY   YAWN

Across

[2] The center of an apple

[4] Big breath when you are tired

Down

[1] Something that is allowed by law is said to be this

[3] The sky is clear and bright on this type of day

Crossword Connection 27

Solve the following puzzle based on the clues given!

DRAG   FIT   APRICOT   SIP

Across

[1] Pull something along the ground

[3] Drink slowly with small mouthfuls

[4] Exercise makes you ... and healthy

Down

[2] A pale orange-coloured stone fruit

Crossword Connection 28

Solve the following puzzle based on the clues given!

RAY   CAB   TOKYO   TEA

Across

[2] A hot beverage made in a pot or in a cup

[3] A beam of sunlight

Down

[1] Taxi

[2] The capital city of Japan

Crossword Connection 29

Solve the following puzzle based on the clues given!

HOT   TENT   STREETS   TOY

Across

[2] A temporary hut you sleep in if you go camping

[4] A red sausage served in bread is a ... dog

Down

[1] Roads where people live

[3] Something you play with

Crossword Connection 30

Solve the following puzzle based on the clues given!

WASH   RINGS   OASIS   NEIGH

Across

[3] The Olympic flag has five of these

[4] When you are dirty you need to do this

Down

[1] A water hole in a desert where trees can grow

[2] The sound a horse makes

Crossword Connection 31

Solve the following puzzle based on the clues given!

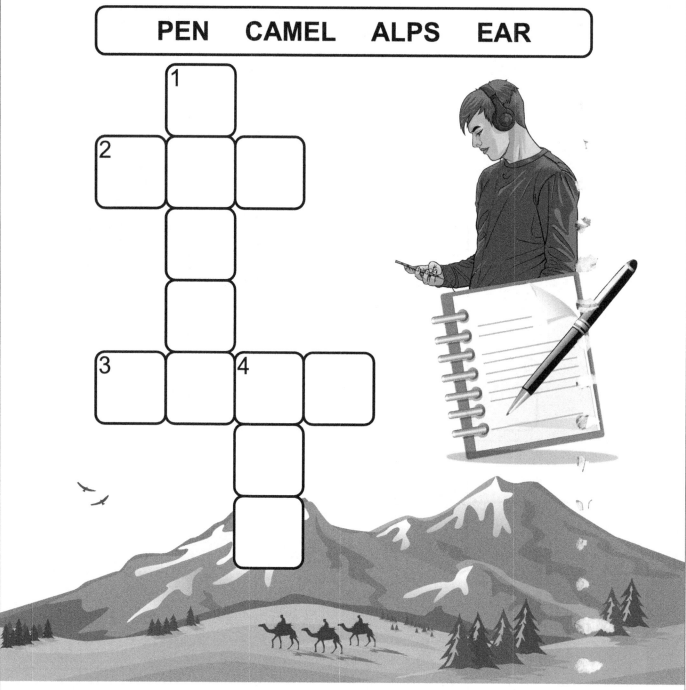

PEN   CAMEL   ALPS   EAR

Across

[2] You can hear with this
[3] Swiss mountains

Down

[1] An animal with a hump that can go a long time with out a drink of water
[4] This has ink in it and you write with it

Crossword Connection 32

Solve the following puzzle based on the clues given!

PEG   WINGS   FAST   FOE

Across

[2] You have to be very ... to win a running race

[3] This is used to hang something on the clothesline

Down

[1] Birds have these so they can fly

[2] Another word for an enemy

Crossword Connection 33

Solve the following puzzle based on the clues given!

PUP   GEMS   PLUS   RED

Across

[2] The color of tomatoes
[3] Four ... four equals eight

Down

[1] Another word for jewels
[3] A young dog

Crossword Connection 34

Solve the following puzzle based on the clues given!

HOT   THIRD   ONION   ONE

Across

[3] First, second, ...
[4] Five, four, three, two, ...

Down

[1] Vary warm
[2] This vegetable makes your eyes sting and cry when you peel it

Crossword Connection 35

Solve the following puzzle based on the clues given!

SCARF   TEACHER   RAPID   OPEN

Across

[2] Warm item you wear around your neck

[4] The opposite of closed

Down

[1] Educate or instruct

[3] Very quick

Crossword Connection 36

Solve the following puzzle based on the clues given!

TOAD   ANGEL   SPELL   SWANS

Across

[2] Elegant birds with long necks

[4] Winged heavenly messenger

Down

[1] Large frog-like creature

[3] Write the letters of a word correctly

Crossword Connection 37

Solve the following puzzle based on the clues given!

CHIP   APRIL   STAR   CLAP

Across

[3] The fourth month of the year

[4] A hot fried slice of potato

Down

[1] Twinkling light in the night sky

[2] Applaud

Crossword Connection 38

Solve the following puzzle based on the clues given!

CAGE   DINNER   YOUNG   ROSE

Across

[2] Main meal of the day, taken around evening

[4] A place to keep a bird or guinea pig

Down

[1] The opposite of old

[3] A kind of red colored flower, symbol of love

Crossword Connection 39

Solve the following puzzle based on the clues given!

CHRISTMAS   HUMMINGBIRD   SNOWMAN   WHALE

Across

[3] A bird that can fly backwards

[4] The largest sea mammal

Down

[1] Man made out of snow with carrot nose

[2] A famous festival of December

Crossword Connection 40

Solve the following puzzle based on the clues given!

TAIL   ORANGE   LAMB   FLEA

Across

[2] The wagging part of a puppy

[3] Biting insect that is a pest to cats and dogs

Down

[1] A citrus fruit with color name

[4] A baby sheep is called a...

Crossword Connection 41

Solve the following puzzle based on the clues given!

BOW   BALLOON   FLOSS   CAKE

Across

[2] Sweet baked food, with candles, served on birthdays

[3] Thread you use to clean between your teeth

[4] An ornamental knot made of ribbon

Down

[1] A flexible bag that can be inflated with air

Crossword Connection 42

Solve the following puzzle based on the clues given!

SONGS   RECIPE   CLOWN   PRIZE

Across

[2] A cook's instructions

[4] Poetry and music created for singing are called

Down

[1] An award given to a person or a group of people

[3] A person who paints their face, wears a funny costume, and works at the circus

Crossword Connection 43

Solve the following puzzle based on the clues given!

ICE   BANANA   BEAST   MILK

Across

[1] A white dairy drink

[3] Fairy tale, Beauty and the ...

Down

[2] Frozen water

[3] A long curved yellow fruit

Crossword Connection 44

Solve the following puzzle based on the clues given!

OVEN   BREAKFAST   NIBBLE   PUNCH

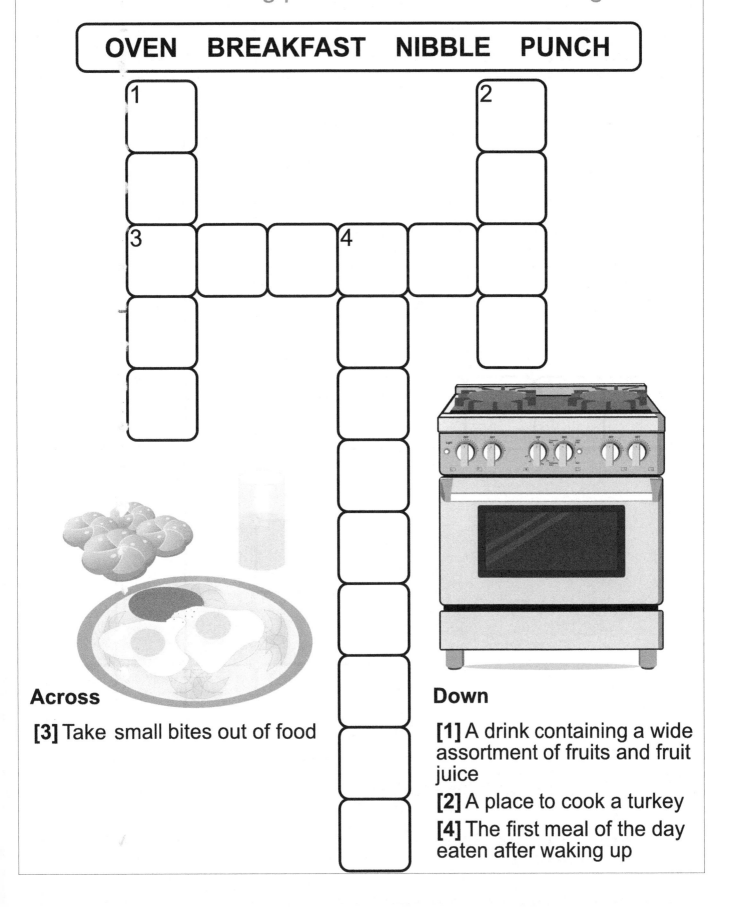

Across

[3] Take small bites out of food

Down

[1] A drink containing a wide assortment of fruits and fruit juice

[2] A place to cook a turkey

[4] The first meal of the day eaten after waking up

Crossword Connection 45

Solve the following puzzle based on the clues given!

PLATTER   DELICIOUS   FEAST   DRUMSTICK

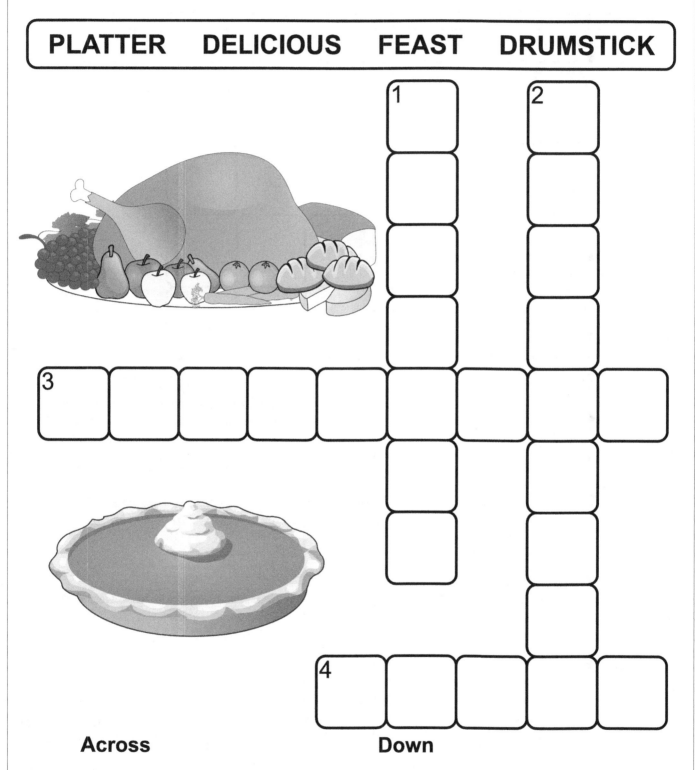

Across

[3] Another word for a turkey leg

[4] A large special meal for many people

Down

[1] One word for large a serving tray

[2] A word to describe very tasty food

Crossword Connection 46

Solve the following puzzle based on the clues given!

SODA   DENTIST   TEETH   TOOTHBRUSH

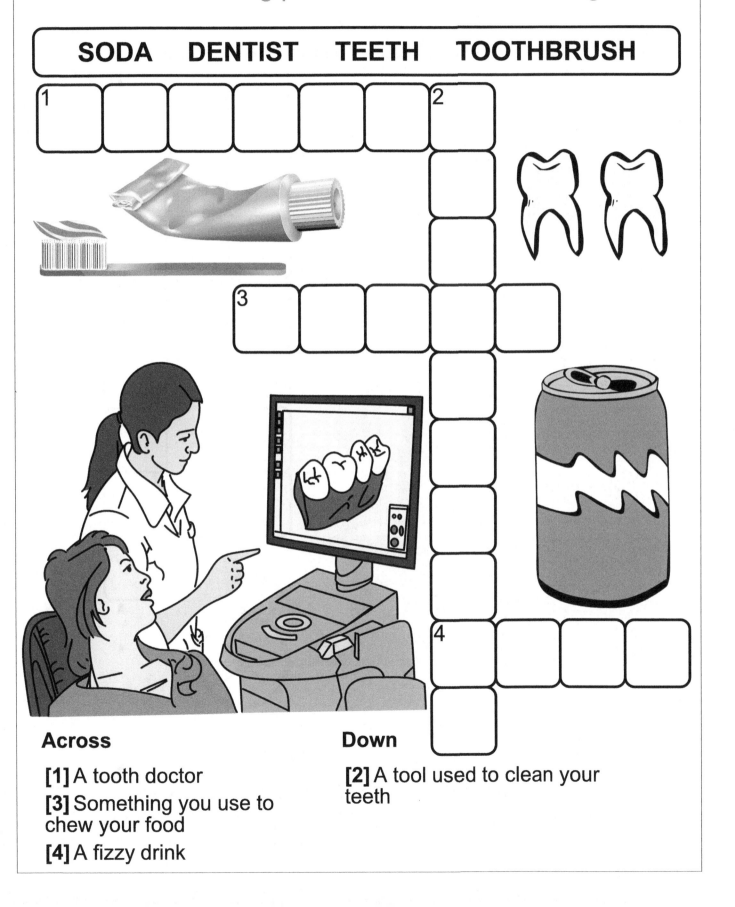

Across

[1] A tooth doctor

[3] Something you use to chew your food

[4] A fizzy drink

Down

[2] A tool used to clean your teeth

Crossword Connection 47

Solve the following puzzle based on the clues given!

STRAW   MUSTARD   NAPKIN   PRETZEL

Across

[2] A yellow sauce for hot dogs
[4] A tube used to drink with

Down

[1] Knot shaped bread
[3] A square paper tissue to wipe your face

Crossword Connection 48

Solve the following puzzle based on the clues given!

PICKLES   MILKSHAKE   SANDWICH   PIZZA

Across

[2] Two slices of bread with some filling between them

[4] Cucumbers preserved in vinegar in a jar

Down

[1] A cold, icy, dairy drink

[3] An Italian bread pie with toppings

Crossword Connection 49

Solve the following puzzle based on the clues given!

FROG   BUTTERFLY   SNAIL   LEAF

Across

[3] Croaking pond-dweller with a sticky tongue

[4] Very slow moving slug like creature with a shell

Down

[1] What a caterpillar becomes

[2] Part of a tree that changes color in the fall

Crossword Connection 50

Solve the following puzzle based on the clues given!

TREE   SQUIRREL   CHERRIES   COCONUT

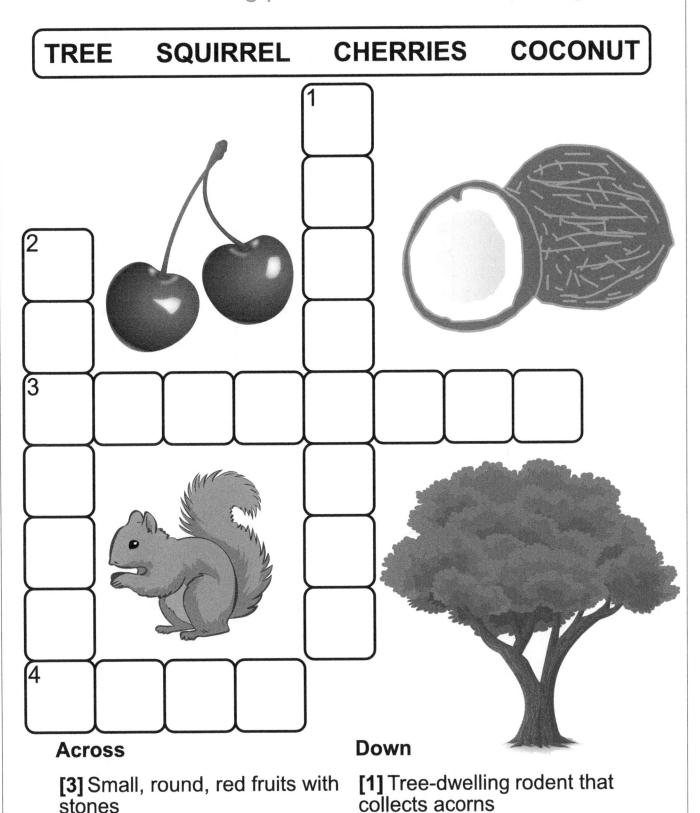

Across

[3] Small, round, red fruits with stones

[4] Tall plant in the forest that squirrel's live in

Down

[1] Tree-dwelling rodent that collects acorns

[2] A food item that grows on palm trees

Crossword Connection 51

Solve the following puzzle based on the clues given!

PEAR GRAPEFRUIT BANANA GRAPES PINEAPPLE

Across

[4] Fruit with a lightbulb shape

[5] Fruit topping for Hawaiian pizza

Down

[1] Small fruits that grow on vines

[2] A long curved yellow fruit.

[3] A large, yellow, sour, fruit

Crossword Connection 52

Solve the following puzzle based on the clues given!

HARMONICA ACCORDION WATERMELON GUITAR STRAWBERRY

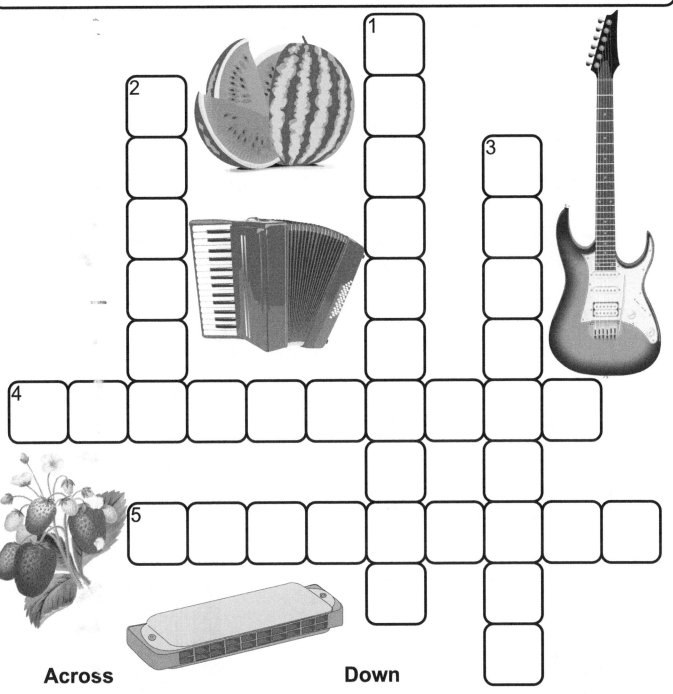

Across

[4] Bright red shortcake fruit

[5] Musical instrument also known as a mouth organ

Down

[1] Very large fruit with green stripes and red on the inside

[2] Rock band electric instrument

[3] A musical instrument, with a keyboard, also known as a squeezebox

Crossword Connection 53

Solve the following puzzle based on the clues given!

VIOLIN   TRUMPET   TAMBOURINE   HARP   PIANO

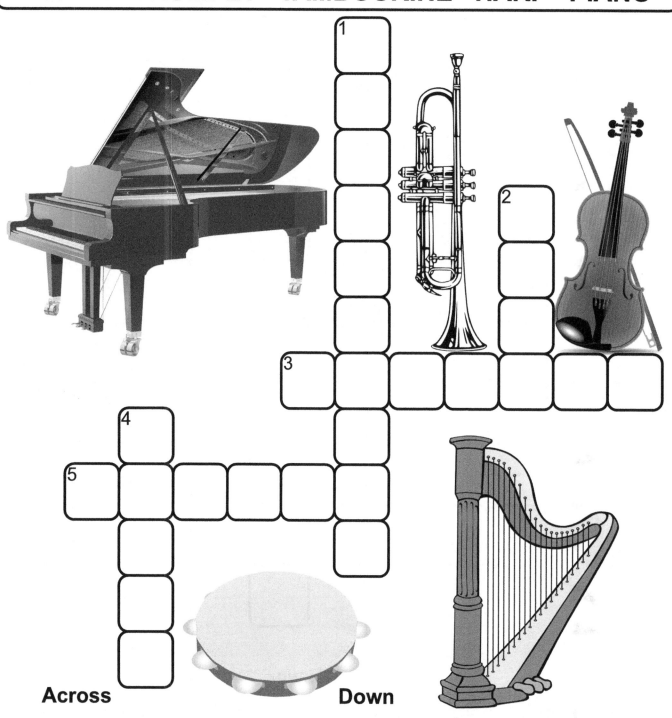

Across

[3] A horn you blow into
[5] Fiddle string instrument

Down

[1] A small shallow jingly drum that you hit with your hand

[2] Angel's music-maker that has 47 strings

[4] Musical instrument with white and black keys

Crossword Connection 54

Solve the following puzzle based on the clues given!

BASEBALL   BADMINTON   BASKETBALL   BOXING   GOLF

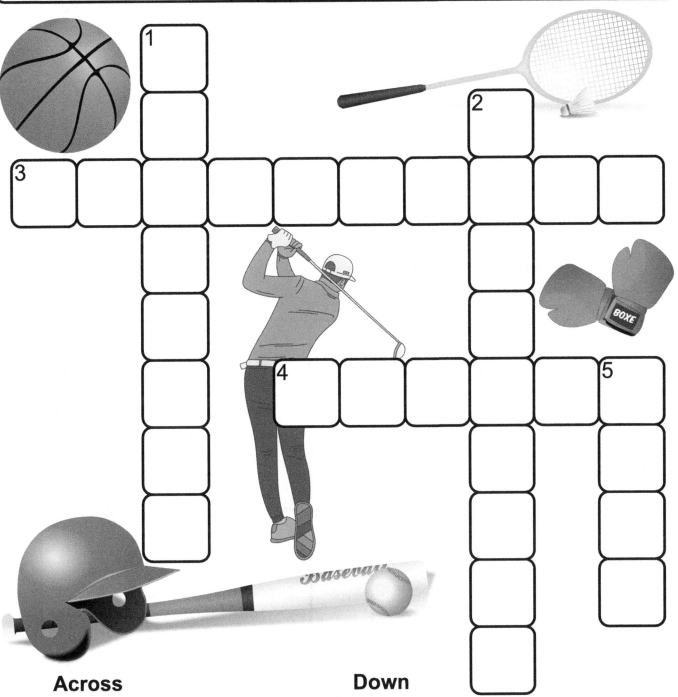

Across

[3] Indoor team sport played with hoops

[4] Sport that involves punching

Down

[1] Game with pitchers, catchers, and hitters

[2] Racket sport played with with birdies and a high net

[5] A walking sport with holes in it

Crossword Connection 55

Solve the following puzzle based on the clues given!

SWIMMING   HIKING   SOCCER   KARATE   SKIING

Across

[3] Ball-kicking game that is called Football in Europe

[4] A fish moving through water is...

Down

[1] Japanese combative sport

[2] Long-distance strenuous walks in the wilds

[3] Going down a snowy hill fast

Crossword Connection 56

Solve the following puzzle based on the clues given!

TENNIS   FISHING   SHRIMP   VOLLEYBALL

Across

[2] Played with rackets on a court with a net touching the middle of it

[4] A lake sport using a rod and reel

Down

[1] Popular beach sport played with a ball and a net

[3] Small sea-creature served on a seafood platter

Crossword Connection 57

Solve the following puzzle based on the clues given!

BEET   DOLPHIN   SHARK   OYSTER   BROCOCOLI

Across

[2] Dangerous sea creature

[3] A purplish red-skinned vegetable

[5] Green vegetable with a flowering head

Down

[1] Shellfish that some times has a pearl in it

[4] 'Smiling' sociable sea mammal who is a relative of the porpoise

Crossword Connection 58

Solve the following puzzle based on the clues given!

CABBAGE   CUCUMBER   CLAM   GARLIC   CORN

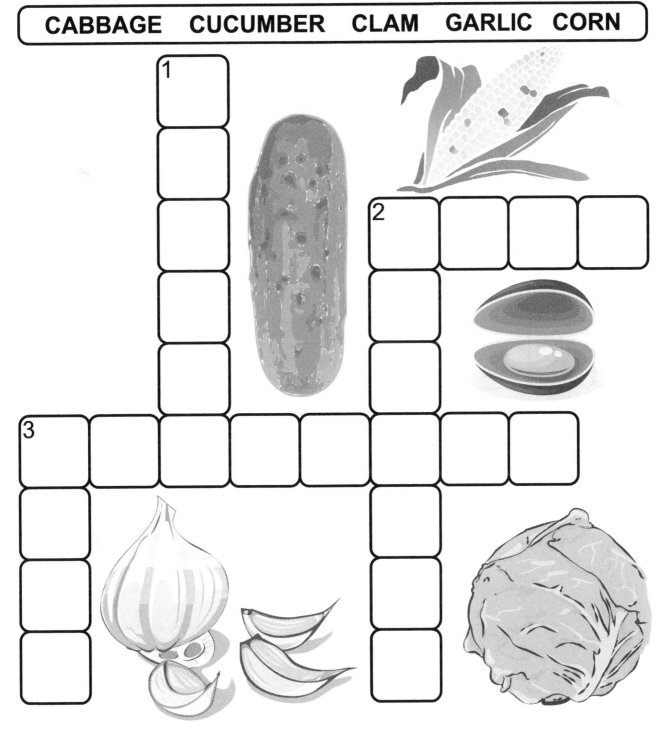

Across

[2] It has a hinged shell

[3] A long green fruit good for salads

Down

[1] A strong smelling herb that is chopped up and used in cooking

[2] A green leaf vegetable

[3] Cob with yellow kernels

Crossword Connection 59

Solve the following puzzle based on the clues given!

GRANDMA   BREAD   SHIP   PUMPKIN   AUTUMN

Across

[4] What toast is made of
[5] A Halloween vegetable

Down

[1] Season when leaves fall
[2] A big boat that travels the ocean
[3] She's a senior family member sometimes called Nanna

Crossword Connection 60

Solve the following puzzle based on the clues given!

POT   PIE   VISIT   WINTER   SIMMER

1
2
3
4
5

Across

[2] A round dessert with a crust that is cut into slices

[4] Heat gently just below boiling point

[5] It can be used for cooking stew

Down

[1] Coldest season of the year

[3] Sometimes friends come over to ...

Crossword Connection 61

Solve the following puzzle based on the clues given!

MOM   SALAD   LOLLIPOP   CARD   HUGS

Across

[4] It can be dressed and tossed

[5] She is sometimes called my mother

Down

[1] Loving squeezes

[2] Round sweet on a stick

[3] A birthday greeting sent in the mail

Crossword Connection 62

Solve the following puzzle based on the clues given!

STARFISH   SEASHELL   FLOWERS   CRAB   OCTOPUS

Across

[1] Plant's that bloom

[4] Sea creature that has a hard shell and claws

[5] Sea creature with five arms

Down

[2] An ocean creatures hard covering that washes up on the beach

[3] Eight-limbed sea creature

Crossword Connection 63

Solve the following puzzle based on the clues given!

CHEESE SALAMI TURTLE HAM PUDDING

Across

[2] A soft, sweet dessert, cooked and served in a bowl

[3] Food such as cheddar and mozzarella

[5] Meat found on a Hawaiian pizza

Down

[1] A slow moving creature that lives in a shell

[4] A spicy cold sausage slice from the deli

Crossword Connection 64

Solve the following puzzle based on the clues given!

ART   SWIMSUIT   POPSICLE   LIFEGUARD   SURFING

Across

[4] Rescuer at a beach or swimming pool

[5] Riding the waves

Down

[1] Frozen fruit-flavored sweet on a stick

[2] Beachwear item

[3] Creative works by painters

Crossword Connection 65

Solve the following puzzle based on the clues given!

SHORTS   SAND   VACATION   SUNSCREEN   SEAGULL

Across

[3] Pants for summer

[4] What the beach is covered with

[5] Tanning lotion

Down

[1] Another name for a holiday

[2] Noisy ocean bird

Crossword Connection 66

Solve the following puzzle based on the clues given!

BROTHER   BABY   AUNT   OCEAN   FAN

Across

[1] A very young child
[2] Your daddy's sister
[4] A place for surfing

Down

[1] If you are his sister he's your ...
[3] Spinner for cooling

Crossword Connection 67

Solve the following puzzle based on the clues given!

SISTER   COUSIN   PARENTS   FAMILY   MUSIC

Across

[3] Mom, dad, and the children are a ...

[4] If you are her brother she is your ...

[5] Your uncle's or aunt's child is your ...

Down

[1] Pleasant sounds from notes

[2] Your mother and father are your ...

Crossword Connection 68

Solve the following puzzle based on the clues given!

CLOUDS TORNADO HURRICANE DRIZZLE UNCLE

Across

[2] They float through the sky and bring us rain

[3] Very fine light rain

[4] A violent spinning storm sometimes called a twister

[5] Your mother's brother is your ...

Down

[1] A big storm with violent wind

Crossword Connection 69

Solve the following puzzle based on the clues given!

CAN   RAIN   TEMPERATURE   TAG   BAT

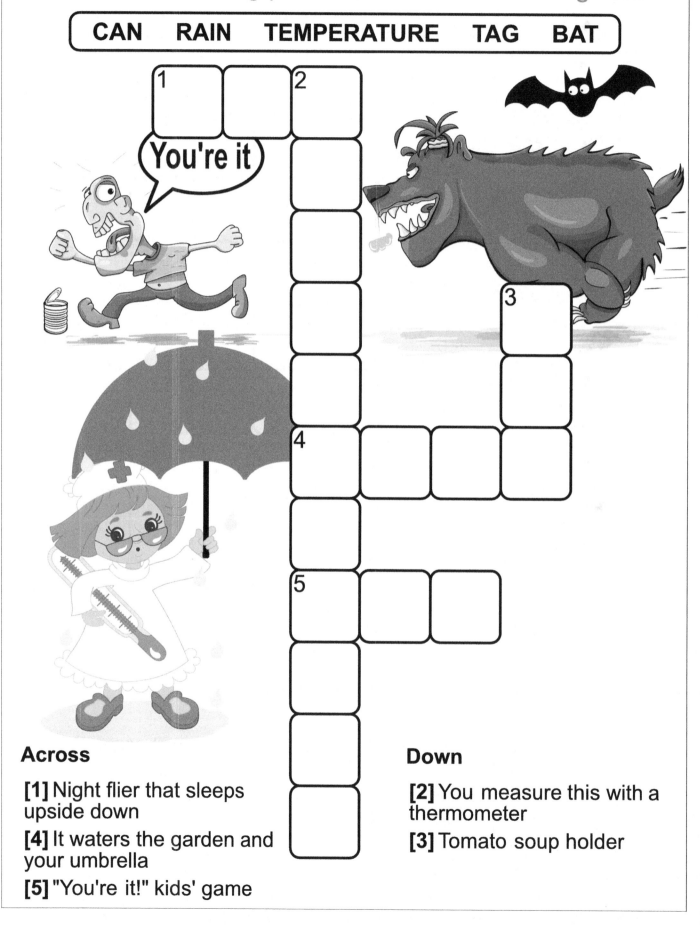

Across

[1] Night flier that sleeps upside down

[4] It waters the garden and your umbrella

[5] "You're it!" kids' game

Down

[2] You measure this with a thermometer

[3] Tomato soup holder

Crossword Connection 70

Solve the following puzzle based on the clues given!

CAT   RAINBOW   LIGHTNING   BAG   HAT

Across

[2] A rabbit may be pulled out of one

[3] Purring furball

[4] A arch of colours during or after it rains

[5] Where to put groceries

Down

[1] An electric charge released between the ground and a cloud

Crossword Connection 71

Solve the following puzzle based on the clues given!

THUNDER WIND SNOWFLAKES BEES BLOSSOM

Across

[4] A stream of air is called ...

[5] Cold crystals that fall to the eath in winter

Down

[1] What you hear after lightning strikes

[2] They live in a hive

[3] What flowers do in the spring

Crossword Connection 72

Solve the following puzzle based on the clues given!

GRASS   GREEN   BREEZE   EGGS   LADYBUG

Across

[1] A small, round, brightly colored and spotted beetle

[5] The color of a lawn

Down

[2] A light wind

[3] It's green and you mow it

[4] Where chickens come from

Crossword Connection 73

Solve the following puzzle based on the clues given!

PICNIC   PUDDLE   SHOWER   HATCH   SPRING

Across

[3] Come out of the egg
[5] Small pool of water

Down

[1] Meal eaten outside
[2] Brief spells of rain
[4] The season before summer

Crossword Connection 74

Solve the following puzzle based on the clues given!

WORM   TULIP   UMBRELLA   THAW   SUNSHINE

Across

[2] Daylight
[4] The early bird gets the ...
[5] Bright spring flower

Down

[1] Melt or unfreeze
[3] It can keep rain off people

Crossword Connection 75

Solve the following puzzle based on the clues given!

CAMPER BACKPACK CAMERA BINOCULARS FIRE

Across

[2] Where there is smoke there is ...

[3] A bag with straps that go over the shoulders

[5] Holiday vehicle

Down

[1] Bird-watcher's glasses

[4] It takes photos

Crossword Connection 76

Solve the following puzzle based on the clues given!

LANTERN   KNIFE   FLASHLIGHT   GLOVES   MOSQUITO

Across

[2] We put them on our hands in the winter

[3] Bloodsucking insect

[5] Some times we use this in stead of a flashlight

Down

[1] We bring this so we can see at night

[4] We use this to cut food

Crossword Connection 77

Solve the following puzzle based on the clues given!

ROPE   COW   CHICKEN   BARBEQUE   RACOON

Across

[3] A Black-masked animal with a bushy ringed tail

[4] A farm bird

Down

[1] Outdoor cooking and grilling

[2] What a lasso is made from

[4] It goes moo

Crossword Connection 78

Solve the following puzzle based on the clues given!

DONKEY   BULL   ROOSTER   PEANUT   ELEPHANT   DOG

Across

[1] Male chicken that crows
[3] Mule
[5] Jelly and ... butter

Down

[2] A very large animal that has a trunk
[3] Pet that barks
[4] A male cow

Crossword Connection 79

Solve the following puzzle based on the clues given!

LEPPARD GOAT ZEBRA ALLIGATOR SHEEP KANGAROO

Across

[1] Wild African striped horse

[4] Animal that often has a beard

[5] Animal sheared for wool

[6] This female Australian jumper has a pocket

Down

[2] Related to crocodiles

[3] A light colored, spotted, wild African cat

Crossword Connection 80

Solve the following puzzle based on the clues given!

RHINOCEROS PARROT PEACOCK TIGER LIZARD OSTRICH

Across

[2] The largest member of the cat family

[6] They have thick skin and long horns on their noses

Down

[1] Bird with a huge bright fan-like tail

[3] Caged bird that can talk

[4] Largest bird in the world

[5] Long-bodied reptile

ANSWERS

Crossword Connection 1

Solve the following puzzle based on the clues given!

Across

[3] A flying toy

Down

[1] A type of bed, double ...
[2] You see with these

Crossword Connection 2

Solve the following puzzle based on the clues given!

ALL   YELLOW   EASY

Across

[2] The color of lemons

Down

[1] Everyone
[3] The opposite of difficult

Crossword Connection 3

Solve the following puzzle based on the clues given!

CUB   MOON   COIN

Across

[2] A bit of metal money

Down

[1] This is seen in the sky at night
[2] A baby lion

Crossword Connection 4

Solve the following puzzle based on the clues given!

END   OPEN   COLD

Across

[1] Not warm
[3] Finish

Down

[2] The opposite of shut

ANSWERS

Crossword Connection 5

Solve the following puzzle based on the clues given!

BANK   ARM   DUCK

Across

[2] A place where you can keep your money

Down

[1] Quacking bird

[3] Your hand is on the end of this

Crossword Connection 6

Solve the following puzzle based on the clues given!

ALONE   DEAF   CAMEL

Across

[1] An animal with a hump that lives in the desert

[3] not able to hear

Down

[2] By yourself

Crossword Connection 7

Solve the following puzzle based on the clues given!

FEET   PET   KNEE

Across

[3] These are at the ends of your legs

Down

[1] The joint in the middle of your leg

[2] A domestic animal that you feed and look after

Crossword Connection 8

Solve the following puzzle based on the clues given!

APPLE   PEA   LAMP

Across

[2] Reading light

[3] Tiny round green vegetable

Down

[1] Crunchy fruit with a core

ANSWERS

Crossword Connection 9

Solve the following puzzle based on the clues given!

STOP   ONE   EIGHT

Across

[1] Five, four, three, two, ...

[3] What you must do at a red light

Down

[2] Four plus four

Crossword Connection 10

Solve the following puzzle based on the clues given!

BALL   EAGLE   BIKE

Across

[1] A two-wheeled vehicle with pedals

[3] A bouncy sphere that's fun to kick, hit and catch

Down

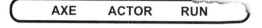

[2] The USA uses the bird as its national emblem

Crossword Connection 11

Solve the following puzzle based on the clues given!

SIREN   POPCORN   NEST

Across

[3] A loud warning sound from an ambulance or firetruck vehicle

Down

[1] A popular snack at the movies

[2] A twig home where a baby bird lives

Crossword Connection 12

Solve the following puzzle based on the clues given!

AXE   ACTOR   RUN

Across

[1] This is used to chop wood

[2] Move quickly

Down

[1] One who likes to pretend

ANSWERS

Crossword Connection 13

Solve the following puzzle based on the clues given!

HOP   STAMP   OAR

```
    ¹S
     T
  ²O A R
     M
  ³H O P
```

Across

[2] A p... ...le used to row a boat
[3] Jump up and down on one foot

Down

[1] You put this on a letter before posting it

Crossword Connection 14

Solve the following puzzle based on the clues given!

SAW   HANDYMAN   WOOD

```
          ¹H
           A
           N
  ²W O O D
           Y
           M
        ³S A W
           N
```

Across

[2] Something you get out of a tree
[3] A wood-cutting tool

Down

[1] A person skilled in doing odd jobs

Crossword Connection 15

Solve the following puzzle based on the clues given!

BEE   CLIMB   BEACH

```
¹B E A C ²C H
 E     L
 F     I
       M
       B
```

Across

[1] Where we go to enjoy the sand and surf

Down

[1] Buzzing insect
[2] Go up a tree, or a hill, or a mountain

Crossword Connection 16

Solve the following puzzle based on the clues given!

APE   WEEKDAY   AGO

```
       ¹W
        E
  ²A P  E
        K
        D
      ³A G O
        Y
```

Across

[2] Large monkey
[3] In the past, a long time ...

Down

[1] Monday, Tuesday, Wednesday, Thursday or Friday

Crossword Connection 17

Solve the following puzzle based on the clues given!

ACORN   YES   LEMON

Across

[3] Sour yellow citrus fruit

Down

[1] The seed of an oak tree
[2] Opposite of no

Crossword Connection 18

Solve the following puzzle based on the clues given!

EEL   BADGE   CAR

Across

[2] Four-wheeled family vehicle
[3] A long slippery fish

Down

[1] You pin this on to your shirt

Crossword Connection 19

Solve the following puzzle based on the clues given!

LID   BOARD   ARM

Across

[2] The part of your body between your shoulder and hand
[3] The top of a jar, bottle or box

Down

[1] Games such as Chess, Scrabble and Ludo are played on one of these

Crossword Connection 20

Solve the following puzzle based on the clues given!

DRUM   CUP   DIRT

Across

[2] An instrument that you hit with sticks to keep the beat

Down

[1] You drink from this
[2] There is lots of this in the garden. It is also called earth

ANSWERS

Crossword Connection 21

Solve the following puzzle based on the clues given!

TIDY   SKI   SNOW

```
          ¹T
   ²S  K  I
      N     D
      O     Y
      W
```

Across

[2] A way to move quickly down a snowy mountainside

Down

[1] Neat and with everything in the right place

[2] In cold places this falls to the ground

Crossword Connection 22

Solve the following puzzle based on the clues given!

SAD   WALLABY   BEAR

```
       ¹W
   ²S  A  D
       L
       L
       A
   ³B  E  A  R
       Y
```

Across

[2] Unhappy

[3] Could be a teddy or a grizzly

Down

[1] A small kangaroo-like animal

Crossword Connection 23

Solve the following puzzle based on the clues given!

ROSE   SEEDS   AISLE

```
      ¹A
      I
   ²R O S E
      L
   ³S E E D S
```

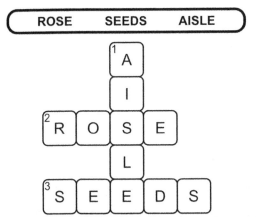

Across

[2] This beautiful flower has thorns on its stem

[3] You plant these to grow flowers or vegetables

Down

[1] The passage between seats in a cinema, church or a walkway in a market

Crossword Connection 24

Solve the following puzzle based on the clues given!

BUS   SCAR   SLUG

```
         ¹B
   ²S  L  U  G
   C     S
   A
   R
```

Across

[2] Slimy slow-moving creature that doesn't have a shell

Down

[1] Something that can take lots of children to school

[2] A mark left on your skin after a wound has healed

ANSWERS

Crossword Connection 25

Solve the following puzzle based on the clues given!

DEEP   ANGEL   BATH

[1]B [2]A T H
A
N
G
[3]D E E P
L

Across

[1] A tub that you fill with water and get in to have a wash

[3] If water in a sink is shallow then water in the bath is...

Down

[2] A heavenly being, or what your mum might call you when you are very good

Crossword Connection 26

Solve the following puzzle based on the clues given!

LEGAL   CORE   SUNNY   YAWN

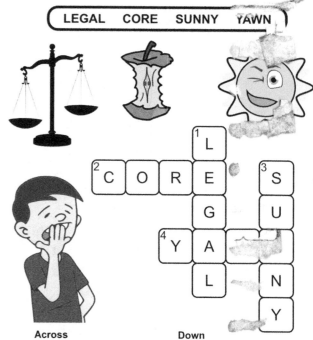

[1]L
[2]C O R E [3]S
E U
G N
[4]Y A N
L Y
Y

Across

[2] The center of an apple

[4] Big breath when you are tired

Down

[1] Something that is allowed by law is said to be this

[3] The sky is clear and bright on this type of day

Crossword Connection 27

Solve the following puzzle based on the clues given!

DRAG   FIT   APRICOT   SIP

[1]D R [2]A G
P
R
[3]S I P
C
O
[4]F I T

Across

[1] Pull something along the ground

[3] Drink slowly with small mouthfuls

[4] Exercise makes you ... and healthy

Down

[2] A pale orange-coloured stone fruit

Crossword Connection 28

Solve the following puzzle based on the clues given!

RAY   CAB   TOKYO   TEA

[1]C
[2]T E
T B
O
K
[3]R A Y
Y
O

Across

[2] A hot beverage made in a pot or in a cup

[3] A beam of sunlight

Down

[1] Taxi

[2] The capital city of Japan

ANSWERS

Crossword Connection 29

Solve the following puzzle based on the clues given!

HOT   TENT   STREETS   TOY

```
    ¹S
  ²T  E  N  ³T
    R        O
    E        Y
    E
 ⁴H O  T
    S
```

Across

[2] A temporary hut you sleep in if you go camping

[4] A red sausage served in bread is a ... dog

Down

[1] Roads where people live

[3] Something you play with

Crossword Connection 30

Solve the following puzzle based on the clues given!

WASH   RINGS   OASIS   NEIGH

```
           ¹O
           A
     ²N    S
     E     I
   ³R I N G S
     G
 ⁴W A S H
```

Across

[3] The Olympic flag has five of these

[4] When you are dirty you need to do this

Down

[1] A water hole in a desert where trees can grow

[2] The sound a horse makes

Crossword Connection 31

Solve the following puzzle based on the clues given!

PEN   CAMEL   ALPS   EAR

```
      ¹C
 ²E A  R
      M
      E
 ³A L ⁴P S
      E
      N
```

Across

[2] You can hear with this

[3] Swiss mountains

Down

[1] An animal with a hump that can go a long time with out a drink of water

[4] This has ink in it and you write with it

Crossword Connection 32

Solve the following puzzle based on the clues given!

PEG   WINGS   FAST   FOE

```
           ¹W
           I
           N
           G
      ²F A S T
      O
    ³P E G
```

Across

[2] You have to be very ... to win a running race

[3] This is used to hang something on the clothesline

Down

[1] Birds have these so they can fly

[2] Another word for an enemy

ANSWERS

Crossword Connection 33

Solve the following puzzle based on the clues given!

PUP   GEMS   PLUS   RED

```
        ¹G
    ²R  E  D
        M
    ³P  L  U  S
    U
    P
```

Across

[2] The color of tomatoes
[3] Four ... four equals eight

Down

[1] Another word for jewels
[3] A young dog

Crossword Connection 34

Solve the following puzzle based on the clues given!

HOT   THIRD   ONION   ONE

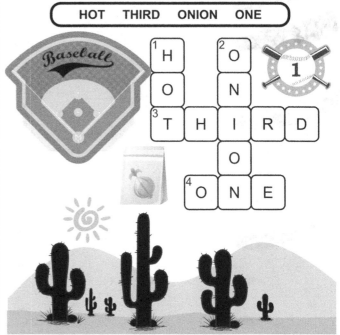

```
    ¹H        ²O
    O         N
    ³T  H  I  R  D
              O
          ⁴O  N  E
```

Across

[3] First, second, ...
[4] Five, four, three, two, ...

Down

[1] Vary warm
[2] This vegetable makes your eyes sting and cry when you peel it

Crossword Connection 35

Solve the following puzzle based on the clues given!

SCARF   TEACHER   RAPID   OPEN

```
        ¹T
        E
        A
    ²S  C  A  ³R  F
        H      A
        ⁴O  P  E  N
               I
               D
```

Across

[2] Warm item you wear around your neck
[4] The opposite of closed

Down

[1] Educate or instruct
[3] Very quick

Crossword Connection 36

Solve the following puzzle based on the clues given!

TOAD   ANGEL   SPELL   SWANS

```
            ¹T
            O
    ²S  W  A  N  ³S
            D      P
                   E
        ⁴A  N  G  E  L
                   L
```

Across

[2] Elegant birds with long necks
[4] Winged heavenly messenger

Down

[1] Large frog-like creature
[3] Write the letters of a word correctly

ANSWERS

Crossword Connection 37

Solve the following puzzle based on the clues given!

CHIP   APRIL   STAR   CLAP

Across

[3] The fourth month of the year

[4] A hot fried slice of potato

Down

[1] Twinkling light in the night sky

[2] Applaud

Crossword Connection 38

Solve the following puzzle based on the clues given!

CAGE   DINNER   YOUNG   ROSE

Across

[2] Main meal of the day, taken around evening

[4] A place to keep a bird or guinea pig

Down

[1] The opposite of old

[3] A kind of red colored flower, symbol of love

Crossword Connection 39

Solve the following puzzle based on the clues given!

CHRISTMAS   HUMMINGBIRD   SNOWMAN   WHALE

Across

[3] A bird that can fly backwards

[4] The largest sea mammal

Down

[1] Man made out of snow with carrot nose

[2] A famous festival of December

Crossword Connection 40

Solve the following puzzle based on the clues given!

TAIL   ORANGE   LAMB   FLEA

Across

[2] The wagging part of a puppy

[3] Biting insect that is a pest to cats and dogs

Down

[1] A citrus fruit with color name

[4] A baby sheep is called a...

Crossword Connection 41

Solve the following puzzle based on the clues given!

BOW   BALLOON   FLOSS   CAKE

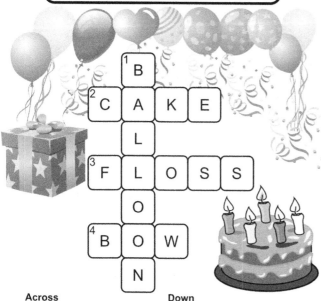

```
        ¹B
   ²C  A  K  E
        L
     ³F  L  O  S  S
        O
   ⁴B  O  W
        N
```

Across

[2] Sweet baked food, with candles, served on birthdays

[3] Thread you use to clean between your teeth

[4] An ornamental knot made of ribbon

Down

[1] A flexible bag that can be inflated with air

Crossword Connection 42

Solve the following puzzle based on the clues given!

SONGS   RECIPE   CLOWN   PRIZE

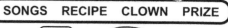
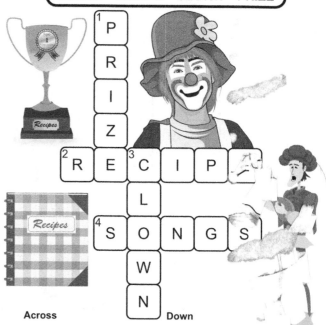

```
        ¹P
        R
        I
        Z
   ²R  E  C  ³I  P  E
        L
   ⁴S  O  N  G  S
        W
        N
```

Across

[2] A cook's instructions

[4] Poetry and music created for singing are called

Down

[1] An award given to a person or a group of people

[3] A person who paints their face, wears a funny costume, and works at the circus

Crossword Connection 43

Solve the following puzzle based on the clues given!

ICE   BANANA   BEAST   MILK

```
   ¹M  ²I  L  K
       C
   ³B  E  A  S  T
   A
   N
   A
   N
   A
```

Across

[1] A white dairy drink

[3] Fairy tale, Beauty and the ...

Down

[2] Frozen water

[3] A long curved yellow fruit

Crossword Connection 44

Solve the following puzzle based on the clues given!

OVEN   BREAKFAST   NIBBLE   PUNCH

```
   ¹P              ²O
   U              V
   ³N  I  B  ⁴B  L  E
   C          R  N
   H          E
              A
              K
              F
              A
              S
              T
```

Across

[3] Take small bites out of food

Down

[1] A drink containing a wide assortment of fruits and fruit juice

[2] A place to cook a turkey

[4] The first meal of the day eaten after waking up

ANSWERS

Crossword Connection 45

Solve the following puzzle based on the clues given!

PLATTER   DELICIOUS   FEAST   DRUMSTICK

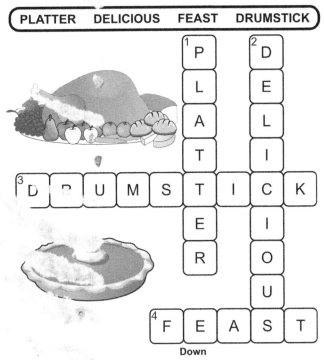

```
      ¹P              ²D
       L               E
       A               L
       T               I
³D  R  U  M  S  T  I  C  K
    D  E               I
       E               O
       R               U
              ⁴F  E  A  S  T
```

Down

[3] Another word for a turkey leg

[4] A large special meal for many p...

[1] One word for large a serving tray

[2] A word to describe very tasty food

Crossword Connection 46

Solve the following puzzle based on the clues given!

SODA   DENTIST   TEETH   TOOTHBRUSH

```
¹D  E  N  T  I  S  T    ²T
                         O
                         O
              ³T  E  E  T  H
                         H
                         B
                         R
                         U
                      ⁴S  O  D  A
                         H
```

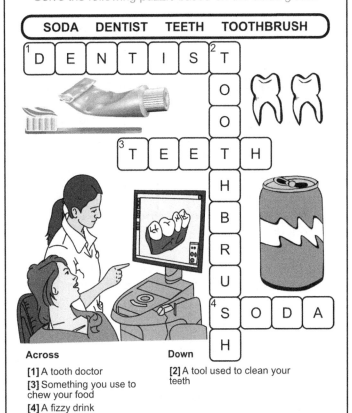

Across

[1] A tooth doctor

[3] Something you use to chew your food

[4] A fizzy drink

Down

[2] A tool used to clean your teeth

Crossword Connection 47

Solve the following puzzle based on the clues given!

STRAW   MUSTARD   NAPKIN   PRETZEL

```
              ¹P
²M  U  S  T  A  R  D
              E       ³N
           ⁴S  T  R  A  W
              Z       P
              E       K
              L       I
                      N
```

Across

[2] A yellow sauce for hot dogs

[4] A tube use... to drink with

Down

[1] Knot shaped bread

[3] A square paper tissue to wipe your face

Crossword Connection 48

Solve the following puzzle based on the clues given!

PICKLES   MILKSHAKE   SANDWICH   PIZZA

```
                      ¹M
²S  A  N  D  W  I  C  H
                      L
        ³P            K
⁴P  I  C  K  L  E  S
        Z             H
        Z             A
        A             K
                      E
```

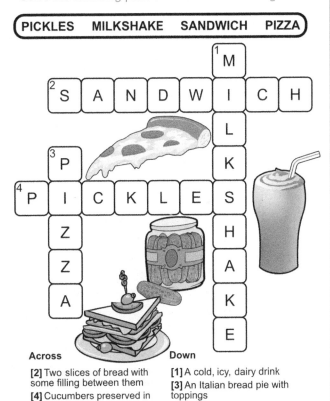

Across

[2] Two slices of bread with some filling between them

[4] Cucumbers preserved in vinegar in a jar

Down

[1] A cold, icy, dairy drink

[3] An Italian bread pie with toppings

ANSWERS

Crossword Connection 49

Solve the following puzzle based on the clues given!

FROG   BUTTERFLY   SNAIL   LEAF

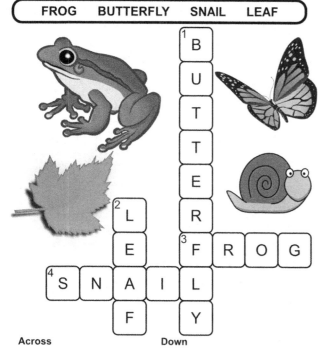

```
            ¹B
            U
            T
            T
            E
     ²L      R
     E    ³F R O G
⁴S N A I L
     F
```

Across

[3] Croaking pond-dweller with a sticky tongue
[4] Very slow moving slug like creature with a shell

Down

[1] What a caterpillar becomes
[2] Part of a tree that changes color in the fall

Crossword Connection 50

Solve the following puzzle based on the clues given!

TREE   SQUIRREL   CHERRIES   COCONUT

```
              ¹S
              Q
   ²C          U
   O          I
   ³C H E R R I E S
   O          R
   N          E
   U          L
   ⁴T R E E
```

Across

[3] Small, round, red fruits with stones
[4] Tall plant in the forest that squirrel's live in

Down

[1] Tree-dwelling rodent that collects acorns
[2] A food item that grows on palm trees

Crossword Connection 51

Solve the following puzzle based on the clues given!

PEAR   GRAPEFRUIT   BANANA   GRAPES   PINEAPPLE

```
                    ¹G
                    R
                    A
       ²B   ³G      ⁴P E A R
       A    R       L
⁵P I N E A P P L E  E
       A    P       S
       N    E
       A    F
            R
            U
            I
            T
```

Across

[4] Fruit with a lightbulb shape
[5] Fruit topping for Hawaiian pizza

Down

[1] Small fruits that grow on vines
[2] A long curved yellow fruit.
[3] A large, yellow, sour, fruit

Crossword Connection 52

Solve the following puzzle based on the clues given!

HARMONICA ACCORDION WATERMELON GUITAR STRAWBERRY

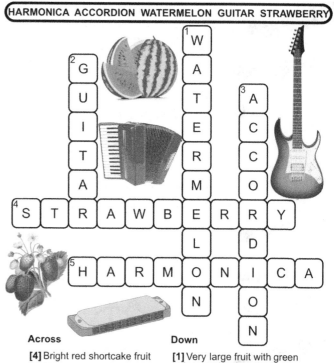

```
              ¹W
   ²G         A
   U          T        ³A
   I          E        C
   T          R        C
   A          M        O
⁴S T R A W B E R R Y
              L        O
   ⁵H A R M O N I C A
              N        O
                       N
```

Across

[4] Bright red shortcake fruit
[5] Musical instrument also known as a mouth organ

Down

[1] Very large fruit with green stripes and red on the inside
[2] Rock band electric instrument
[3] A musical instrument, with a keyboard, also known as a squeezebox

ANSWERS

Crossword Connection 53

Solve the following puzzle based on the clues given!

VIOLIN TRUMPET TAMBOURINE HARP PIANO

Grid answers:
- 1 Down: TAMBOURINE
- 2 Down: HARP
- 3 Across: TRUMPET
- 4 Down: PIANO
- 5 Across: VIOLIN

Across

[3] A horn you blow into
[5] Fiddle string instrument

Down

[1] A small shallow jingly drum that you hit with your hand
[2] Angel's music-maker that has 47 strings
[4] Musical instrument with white and black keys

Crossword Connection 54

Solve the following puzzle based on the clues given!

BASEBALL BADMINTON BASKETBALL BOXING GOLF

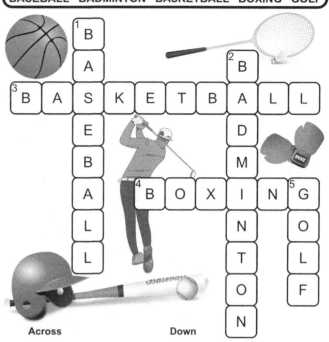

Grid answers:
- 1 Down: BASEBALL
- 2 Down: BADMINTON
- 3 Across: BASKETBALL
- 4 Across: BOXING
- 5 Down: GOLF

Across

[3] Indoor team sport played with hoops
[4] Sport that involves punching

Down

[1] Game with pitchers, catchers, and hitters
[2] Racket sport played with birdies and a high net
[5] A walking sport with holes in it

Crossword Connection 55

Solve the following puzzle based on the clues given!

SWIMMING HIKING SOCCER KARATE SKIING

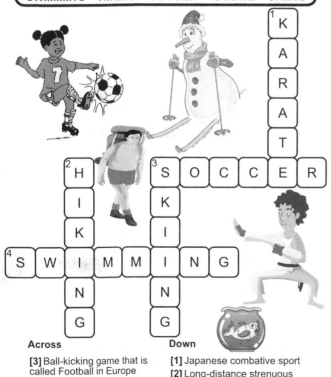

Grid answers:
- 1 Down: KARATE
- 2 Down: HIKING
- 3 Down: SKIING
- 3 Across: SOCCER
- 4 Across: SWIMMING

Across

[3] Ball-kicking game that is called Football in Europe
[4] A fish moving through water is...

Down

[1] Japanese combative sport
[2] Long-distance strenuous walks in the wilds
[3] Going down a snowy hill fast

Crossword Connection 56

Solve the following puzzle based on the clues given!

TENNIS FISHING SHRIMP VOLLEYBALL

Grid answers:
- 1 Down: VOLLEYBALL
- 2 Across: TENNIS
- 3 Down: SHRIMP
- 4 Across: FISHING

Across

[2] Played with rackets on a court with a net touching the middle of it
[4] A lake sport using a rod and reel

Down

[1] Popular beach sport played with a ball and a net
[3] Small sea-creature served on a seafood platter

ANSWERS

Crossword Connection 57

Solve the following puzzle based on the clues given!

BEET DOLPHIN SHARK OYSTER BROCOCOLI

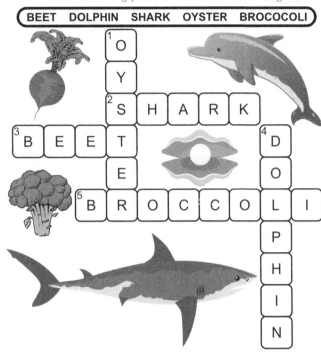

Across

[2] Dangerous sea creature
[3] A purplish red-skinned vegetable
[5] Green vegetable with a flowering head

Down

[1] Shellfish that some times has a pearl in it
[4] 'Smiling' sociable sea mammal who is a relative of the porpoise

Crossword Connection 58

Solve the following puzzle based on the clues given!

CABBAGE CUCUMBER CLAM GARLIC CORN

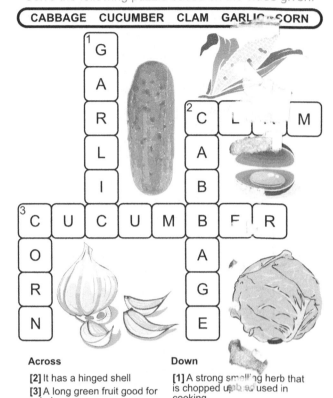

Across

[2] It has a hinged shell
[3] A long green fruit good for salads

Down

[1] A strong smelling herb that is chopped up and used in cooking
[2] A green leaf vegetable
[3] Cob with yellow kernels

Crossword Connection 59

Solve the following puzzle based on the clues given!

GRANDMA BREAD SHIP PUMPKIN AUTUMN

Across

[4] What toast is made of
[5] A Halloween vegetable

Down

[1] Season when leaves fall
[2] A big boat that travels the ocean
[3] She's a senior family member sometimes called Nanna

Crossword Connection 60

Solve the following puzzle based on the clues given!

POT PIE VISIT WINTER SIMMER

Across

[2] A round dessert with a crust that is cut into slices
[4] Heat gently just below boiling point
[5] It can be used for cooking stew

Down

[1] Coldest season of the year
[3] Sometimes friends come over to ...

ANSWERS

Crossword Connection 61

Solve the following puzzle based on the clues given!

MOM   SALAD   LOLLIPOP   CARD   HUGS

	¹H		²L		³C	
	U		O		A	
	G		L		R	
⁴S	A	L	A	D
			I			
			P			
		⁵M	O	M		
			P			

Across

[4] It can be dressed and tossed

... is sometimes called ...

Down

[1] Loving squeezes

[2] Round sweet on a stick

[3] A birthday greeting sent in the mail

Crossword Connection 62

Solve the following puzzle based on the clues given!

STARFISH   SEASHELL   FLOWERS   CRAB   OCTOPUS

¹F L O W E R S ²S
E
³O ⁴C R A B
C S
⁵S T A R F I S H
T E
O L
P L
U
S

Across

[1] Plant's that bloom

[4] Sea creature that has a hard shell and claws

[5] Sea creature with five arms

Down

[2] An ocean creatures hard covering that washes up on the beach

[3] E... limbed sea creature

Crossword Connection 63

Solve the following puzzle based on the clues given!

CHEESE   SALAMI   TURTLE   HAM   PUDDING

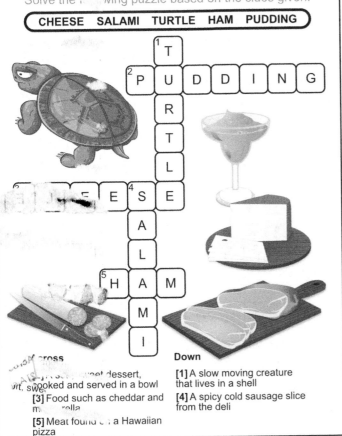

¹T
²P U D D I N G
U
R
T
L
E
⁶... E E S E ⁴S
A
L
⁵H A M
M
I

Across

... sweet dessert, ... snooked and served in a bowl

[3] Food such as cheddar and mozzarella

[5] Meat found on a Hawaiian pizza

Down

[1] A slow moving creature that lives in a shell

[4] A spicy cold sausage slice from the deli

Crossword Connection 64

Solve the following puzzle based on the clues given!

ART   SWIMSUIT   POPSICLE   LIFEGUARD   SURFING

¹P
O
P
S
²S I
W C
⁴L I F E G U A R D
M E ³A
⁵S U R F I N G R
U T
I
T

Across

[4] Rescuer at a beach or swimming pool

[5] Riding the waves

Down

[1] Frozen fruit-flavored sweet on a stick

[2] Beachwear item

[3] Creative works by painters

ANSWERS

Crossword Connection 65

Solve the following puzzle based on the clues given!

SHORTS   SAND   VACATION   SUNSCREEN   SEAGULL

Across

[3] Pants for summer
[4] What the beach is covered with
[5] Tanning lotion

Down

[1] Another name for a holiday
[2] Noisy ocean bird

Crossword Connection 66

Solve the following puzzle based on the clues given!

BROTHER   BABY   AUNT   OCEAN   FAN

Across

[1] A very young child
[2] Your daddy's sister
[4] A place for surfing

Down

[1] If you are his sister he's your ...
[3] Spinner for cooling

Crossword Connection 67

Solve the following puzzle based on the clues given!

SISTER   COUSIN   PARENTS   FAMILY   MUSIC

Across

[3] Mom, dad, and the children are a ...
[4] If you are her brother she is your ...
[5] Your uncle's or aunt's child is your ...

Down

[1] Pleasant sounds from notes
[2] Your mother and father are your ...

Crossword Connection 68

Solve the following puzzle based on the clues given!

CLOUDS   TORNADO   HURRICANE   DRIZZLE   UNCLE

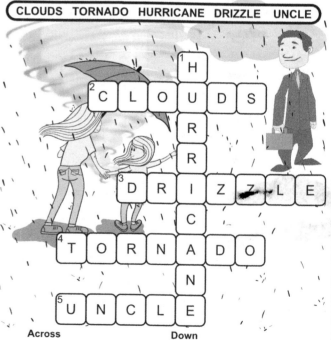

Across

[2] They float through the sky and bring us rain
[3] Very fine light rain
[4] A violent spinning storm sometimes called a twister
[5] Your mother's brother is your ...

Down

[1] A big storm with violent wind

ANSWERS

Crossword Connection 69

Solve the following puzzle based on the clues given!

CAN   RAIN   TEMPERATURE   TAG   BAT

You're it

```
B  A  T     T
            E
            M
            P       C
            E       A
            R  A  I  N
            A
            T  A  G
            U
            R
            E
```

Across

[1] Night flier that sleeps upside down
[4] It waters the garden and your umbrella
[5] "You're it!" kids' game

Down

[2] You measure this with a thermometer
[3] Tomato soup holder

Crossword Connection 70

Solve the following puzzle based on the clues given!

CAT   RAINBOW   LIGHTNING   BAG   HAT

```
         L
         I
         G
         H  A  T
C  A  T  T
         N
R  A  I  N  B  O  W
         I
         N
B  A  G
```

Across

[2] A rabbit may be pulled out of one
[3] Purring furball
[4] A arch of colours during or after it rains
[5] Where to put groceries

Down

[1] An electric charge released between the ground and a cloud

Crossword Connection 71

Solve the following puzzle based on the clues given!

THUNDER   WIND   SNOWFLAKES   BEES   BLOSSOM

```
                  T
                  H
                  U
B              B  N
E              L  D
E              O
S  N  O  W  F  L  A  K  E  S
               S        E
               S        R
               O
               M
```

Across

[4] A stream of air is called ...
[5] Cold crystals that fall to the eath in winter

Down

[1] What you hear after lightning strikes
[2] They live in a hive
[3] What flowers do in the spring

Crossword Connection 72

Solve the following puzzle based on the clues given!

GRASS   GREEN   BREEZE   EGGS   LADYBUG

```
L  A  D  Y  B  U  G
         R     R
         E     A
E        E     S
G        Z     S
G  R  E  E  N
S
```

Across

[1] A small, round, brightly colored and spotted beetle
[5] The color of a lawn

Down

[2] A light wind
[3] It's green and you mow it
[4] Where chickens come from

ANSWERS

Crossword Connection 73

Solve the following puzzle based on the clues given!

PICNIC PUDDLE SHOWER HATCH SPRING

Across
- [3] Come out of the egg
- [5] Small pool of water

Down
- [1] Meal eaten outside
- [2] Brief spells of rain
- [4] The season before summer

Crossword Connection 74

Solve the following puzzle based on the clues given!

WORM TULIP UMBRELLA THAW ~~WO~~ SHINE

Across
- [2] Daylight
- [4] The early bird gets the ...
- [5] Bright spring flower

Down
- [1] Melt or unfreeze
- [3] It can keep rain off

Crossword Connection 75

Solve the following puzzle based on the clues given!

CAMPER BACKPACK CAMERA BINOCULARS FIRE

Across
- [2] Where there is smoke there is ...
- [3] A bag with straps that go over the shoulders
- [5] Holiday vehicle

Down
- [1] Bird-watcher's glasses
- [4] It takes photos

Crossword Connection 76

Solve the following puzzle based on the clues given!

LANTERN KNIFE FLASHLIGHT GLOVES

Across
- [2] We put them on our hands in the winter
- [3] Bloodsucking insect
- [5] Some times we use this in stead of a flashlight

Down
- [1] We bring this so we can see at night
- [4] We use this to cut food

ANSWERS

Crossword Connection 77

Solve the following puzzle based on the clues given!

ROPE ___ CHICKEN BARBEQUE RACOON

Across

[3] A Black-masked animal with a bushy ringed tail
[4] A ___

Down

[1] Outdoor cooking and grilling
[2] What a lasso is made from
[4] It goes moo

Crossword Connection 78

Solve the following puzzle based on the clues given!

DONKEY BULL ROOSTER PEANUT ELEPHANT DOG

Across

[1] Male chicken that crows
[3] Mule
[5] Jelly and ... butter

Down

[2] A very large animal that has a trunk
[3] Pet that barks
[4] A male cow

Crossword Connection 79

Solve the following puzzle based on the clues given!

___ OAT ZEBRA ALLIGATOR SHEEP KANGAROO

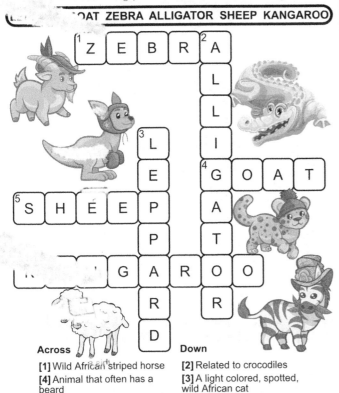

Across

[1] Wild African striped horse
[4] Animal that often has a beard
[5] Animal sheared for wool
[6] This female Australian jumper has a pocket

Down

[2] Related to crocodiles
[3] A light colored, spotted, wild African cat

Crossword Connection 80

Solve the following puzzle based on the clues given!

RHINOCEROS PARROT PEACOCK TIGER LIZARD OSTRICH

Across

[2] The largest member of the cat family
[6] They have thick skin and long horns on their noses

Down

[1] Bird with a huge bright fan-like tail
[3] Caged bird that can talk
[4] Largest bird in the world
[5] Long-bodied reptile

DID YOU KNOW?

WE HAVE AMAZING

You can find all of our books in our Amazon bookstore here:

https://amazon.com/author/jwpublishing